Robert Louis Stevenson (13 November 1850 – 3 December 1894) was a Scottish novelist and travel writer, most noted for Treasure Island, Kidnapped, Strange Case of Dr Jekyll and Mr Hyde, and A Child's Garden of Verses. Born and educated in Edinburgh, Stevenson suffered from serious bronchial trouble for much of his life, but continued to write prolifically and travel widely, in defiance of his poor health. As a young man, he mixed in London literary circles, receiving encouragement from Andrew Lang, Edmund Gosse, Leslie Stephen and W. E. Henley, the last of whom may have provided the model for Long John Silver in Treasure Island. His travels took him to France, America and Australia, before he finally settled in Samoa, where he died. A celebrity in his lifetime, Stevenson attracted a more negative critical response for much of the 20th century, though his reputation has been largely restored. He is currently ranked as the 26th most translated author in the world.(Source: Wikipedia)

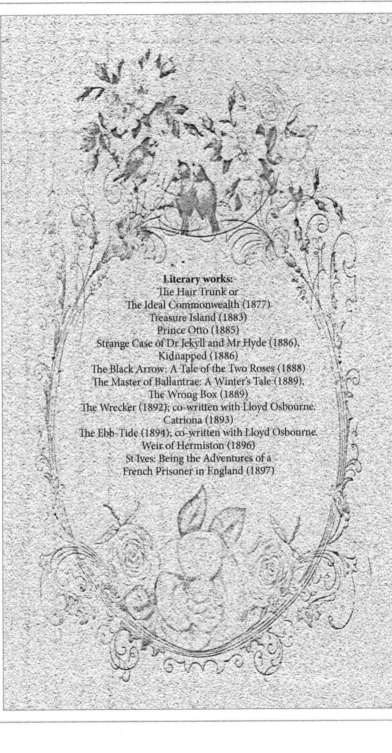

Literary works:
The Hair Trunk or
The Ideal Commonwealth (1877)
Treasure Island (1883)
Prince Otto (1885)
Strange Case of Dr Jekyll and Mr Hyde (1886),
Kidnapped (1886)
The Black Arrow: A Tale of the Two Roses (1888)
The Master of Ballantrae: A Winter's Tale (1889),
The Wrong Box (1889)
The Wrecker (1892); co-written with Lloyd Osbourne.
Catriona (1893)
The Ebb-Tide (1894); co-written with Lloyd Osbourne.
Weir of Hermiston (1896)
St Ives: Being the Adventures of a
French Prisoner in England (1897)

BALLADS
ROBERT LOUIS STEVENSON

PRINCE CLASSICS

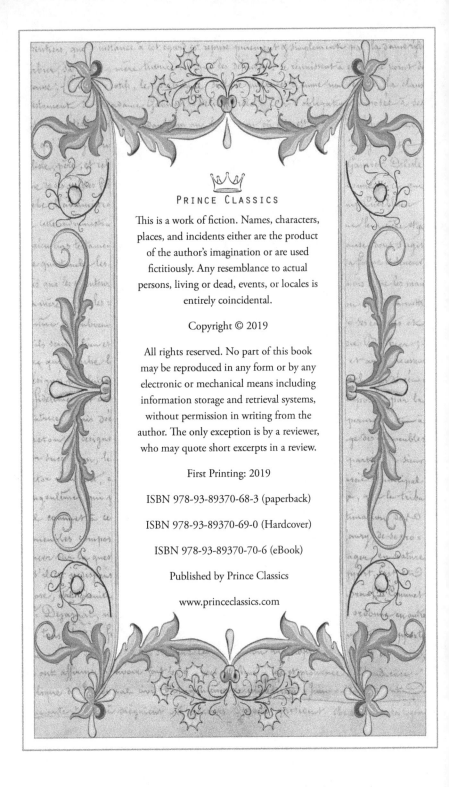

PRINCE CLASSICS

Copyright © 2019

First Printing: 2019

ISBN 978-93-89370-68-3 (paperback)

ISBN 978-93-89370-69-0 (Hardcover)

ISBN 978-93-89370-70-6 (eBook)

Published by Prince Classics

www.princeclassics.com

Contents

BALLADS

THE SONG OF RAHÉRO: A LEGEND OF TAHITI

TO ORI A ORI

Ori, my brother in the island mode,

In every tongue and meaning much my friend,

This story of your country and your clan,

In your loved house, your too much honoured guest,

I made in English. Take it, being done;

And let me sign it with the name you gave.

                                        Teriitera.

I. THE SLAYING OF TÁMATÉA

It fell in the days of old, as the men of Taiárapu tell,

A youth went forth to the fishing, and fortune favoured him well.

Támatéa his name: gullible, simple, and kind,

Comely of countenance, nimble of body, empty of mind,

His mother ruled him and loved him beyond the wont of a wife,

Serving the lad for eyes and living herself in his life.

Alone from the sea and the fishing came Támatéa the fair,

Urging his boat to the beach, and the mother awaited him there,

—"Long may you live!" said she. "Your fishing has sped to a wish.

And now let us choose for the king the fairest of all your fish.

For fear inhabits the palace and grudging grows in the land,

Marked is the sluggardly foot and marked the niggardly hand,

The hours and the miles are counted, the tributes numbered and weighed,

And woe to him that comes short, and woe to him that delayed!"

So spoke on the beach the mother, and counselled the wiser thing.

For Rahéro stirred in the country and secretly mined the king.

Nor were the signals wanting of how the leaven wrought,

In the cords of obedience loosed and the tributes grudgingly brought.

And when last to the temple of Oro the boat with the victim sped,

And the priest uncovered the basket and looked on the face of the dead,

Trembling fell upon all at sight of an ominous thing,

For there was the aito [5] dead, and he of the house of the king.

So spake on the beach the mother, matter worthy of note,

And wattled a basket well, and chose a fish from the boat;

And Támatéa the pliable shouldered the basket and went,

And travelled, and sang as he travelled, a lad that was well content.

Still the way of his going was round by the roaring coast,

Where the ring of the reef is broke and the trades run riot the most.

On his left, with smoke as of battle, the billows battered the land;

Unscalable, turreted mountains rose on the inner hand.

And cape, and village, and river, and vale, and mountain above,

Each had a name in the land for men to remember and love;

And never the name of a place, but lo! a song in its praise:

Ancient and unforgotten, songs of the earlier days,

That the elders taught to the young, and at night, in the full of the moon,

Garlanded boys and maidens sang together in tune.

Támatéa the placable went with a lingering foot;

He sang as loud as a bird, he whistled hoarse as a flute;

He broiled in the sun, he breathed in the grateful shadow of trees,

In the icy stream of the rivers he waded over the knees;

And still in his empty mind crowded, a thousand-fold,

The deeds of the strong and the songs of the cunning heroes of old.

11

And now was he come to a place Taiárapu honoured the most,

Where a silent valley of woods debouched on the noisy coast,

Spewing a level river. There was a haunt of Pai. [7]

There, in his potent youth, when his parents drove him to die,

Honoura lived like a beast, lacking the lamp and the fire,

Washed by the rains of the trade and clotting his hair in the mire;

And there, so mighty his hands, he bent the tree to his foot—

So keen the spur of his hunger, he plucked it naked of fruit.

There, as she pondered the clouds for the shadow of coming ills,

Ahupu, the woman of song, walked on high on the hills.

Of these was Rahéro sprung, a man of a godly race;

And inherited cunning of spirit and beauty of body and face.

Of yore in his youth, as an aito, Rahéro wandered the land,

Delighting maids with his tongue, smiting men with his hand.

Famous he was in his youth; but before the midst of his life

Paused, and fashioned a song of farewell to glory and strife.

House of mine (it went), house upon the sea,

Belov'd of all my fathers, more belov'd by me!

Vale of the strong Honoura, deep ravine of Pai,

Again in your woody summits I hear the trade-wind cry.

House of mine, in your walls, strong sounds the sea,

Of all sounds on earth, dearest sound to me.

I have heard the applause of men, I have heard it arise and die:

Sweeter now in my house I hear the trade-wind cry.

These were the words of his singing, other the thought of his heart;

For secret desire of glory vexed him, dwelling apart.

Lazy and crafty he was, and loved to lie in the sun,

And loved the cackle of talk and the true word uttered in fun;

Lazy he was, his roof was ragged, his table was lean,

And the fish swam safe in his sea, and he gathered the near and the green.

He sat in his house and laughed, but he loathed the king of the land,

And he uttered the grudging word under the covering hand.

Treason spread from his door; and he looked for a day to come,

A day of the crowding people, a day of the summoning drum,

When the vote should be taken, the king be driven forth in disgrace,

And Rahéro, the laughing and lazy, sit and rule in his place,

Here Támatéa came, and beheld the house on the brook;

And Rahéro was there by the way and covered an oven to cook. [10a]

Naked he was to the loins, but the tattoo covered the lack,

And the sun and the shadow of palms dappled his muscular back.

Swiftly he lifted his head at the fall of the coming feet,

And the water sprang in his mouth with a sudden desire of meat;

For he marked the basket carried, covered from flies and the sun; [10b]

And Rahéro buried his fire, but the meat in his house was done.

Forth he stepped; and took, and delayed the boy, by the hand;

And vaunted the joys of meat and the ancient ways of the land:

—"Our sires of old in Taiárapu, they that created the race,

Ate ever with eager hand, nor regarded season or place,

Ate in the boat at the oar, on the way afoot; and at night

Arose in the midst of dreams to rummage the house for a bite.

It is good for the youth in his turn to follow the way of the sire;

And behold how fitting the time! for here do I cover my fire."

—"I see the fire for the cooking but never the meat to cook,"

Said Támatéa.—"Tut!" said Rahéro. "Here in the brook

And there in the tumbling sea, the fishes are thick as flies,

Hungry like healthy men, and like pigs for savour and size:

Crayfish crowding the river, sea-fish thronging the sea."

—"Well it may be," says the other, "and yet be nothing to me.

Fain would I eat, but alas! I have needful matter in hand,

Since I carry my tribute of fish to the jealous king of the land."

Now at the word a light sprang in Rahéro's eyes.

"I will gain me a dinner," thought he, "and lend the king a surprise."

And he took the lad by the arm, as they stood by the side of the track,

And smiled, and rallied, and flattered, and pushed him forward and back.

It was "You that sing like a bird, I never have heard you sing,"

And "The lads when I was a lad were none so feared of a king.

And of what account is an hour, when the heart is empty of guile?

But come, and sit in the house and laugh with the women awhile;

And I will but drop my hook, and behold! the dinner made."

So Támatéa the pliable hung up his fish in the shade

On a tree by the side of the way; and Rahéro carried him in,

Smiling as smiles the fowler when flutters the bird to the gin,

And chose him a shining hook, [13] and viewed it with sedulous eye,

And breathed and burnished it well on the brawn of his naked thigh,

And set a mat for the gull, and bade him be merry and bide,

Like a man concerned for his guest, and the fishing, and nothing beside.

Now when Rahéro was forth, he paused and hearkened, and heard

The gull jest in the house and the women laugh at his word;

And stealthily crossed to the side of the way, to the shady place

Where the basket hung on a mango; and craft transfigured his face.

Deftly he opened the basket, and took of the fat of the fish,

The cut of kings and chieftains, enough for a goodly dish.

This he wrapped in a leaf, set on the fire to cook

15

And buried; and next the marred remains of the tribute he took,

And doubled and packed them well, and covered the basket close

—"There is a buffet, my king," quoth he, "and a nauseous dose!"—

And hung the basket again in the shade, in a cloud of flies

—"And there is a sauce to your dinner, king of the crafty eyes!"

Soon as the oven was open, the fish smelt excellent good.

In the shade, by the house of Rahéro, down they sat to their food,

And cleared the leaves [14] in silence, or uttered a jest and laughed,

And raising the cocoanut bowls, buried their faces and quaffed.

But chiefly in silence they ate; and soon as the meal was done,

Rahéro feigned to remember and measured the hour by the sun,

And "Támatéa," quoth he, "it is time to be jogging, my lad."

So Támatéa arose, doing ever the thing he was bade,

And carelessly shouldered the basket, and kindly saluted his host;

And again the way of his going was round by the roaring coast.

Long he went; and at length was aware of a pleasant green,

And the stems and shadows of palms, and roofs of lodges between

There sate, in the door of his palace, the king on a kingly seat,

And aitos stood armed around, and the yottowas [16] sat at his feet.

But fear was a worm in his heart: fear darted his eyes;

And he probed men's faces for treasons and pondered their speech for lies.

To him came Támatéa, the basket slung in his hand,

And paid him the due obeisance standing as vassals stand.

In silence hearkened the king, and closed the eyes in his face,

Harbouring odious thoughts and the baseless fears of the base;

In silence accepted the gift and sent the giver away.

So Támatéa departed, turning his back on the day.

And lo! as the king sat brooding, a rumour rose in the crowd;

The yottowas nudged and whispered, the commons murmured aloud;

Tittering fell upon all at sight of the impudent thing,

At the sight of a gift unroyal flung in the face of a king.

And the face of the king turned white and red with anger and shame

In their midst; and the heart in his body was water and then was flame;

Till of a sudden, turning, he gripped an aito hard,

A youth that stood with his ómare, [17] one of the daily guard,

And spat in his ear a command, and pointed and uttered a name,

And hid in the shade of the house his impotent anger and shame.

Now Támatéa the fool was far on the homeward way,

The rising night in his face, behind him the dying day.

Rahéro saw him go by, and the heart of Rahéro was glad,

Devising shame to the king and nowise harm to the lad;

And all that dwelt by the way saw and saluted him well,

For he had the face of a friend and the news of the town to tell;

And pleased with the notice of folk, and pleased that his journey was done,

Támatéa drew homeward, turning his back to the sun.

And now was the hour of the bath in Taiárapu: far and near

The lovely laughter of bathers rose and delighted his ear.

Night massed in the valleys; the sun on the mountain coast

Struck, end-long; and above the clouds embattled their host,

And glowed and gloomed on the heights; and the heads of the palms were gems,

And far to the rising eve extended the shade of their stems;

And the shadow of Támatéa hovered already at home.

And sudden the sound of one coming and running light as the foam

Struck on his ear; and he turned, and lo! a man on his track,

Girded and armed with an ómare, following hard at his back.

At a bound the man was upon him;—and, or ever a word was said,

The loaded end of the ómare fell and laid him dead.

II. THE VENGING OF TÁMATÉA

Thus was Rahéro's treason; thus and no further it sped
The king sat safe in his place and a kindly fool was dead.

But the mother of Támatéa arose with death in her eyes.

All night long, and the next, Taiárapu rang with her cries.

As when a babe in the wood turns with a chill of doubt

And perceives nor home, nor friends, for the trees have closed her about,

The mountain rings and her breast is torn with the voice of despair:

So the lion-like woman idly wearied the air

For awhile, and pierced men's hearing in vain, and wounded their hearts.

But as when the weather changes at sea, in dangerous parts,

And sudden the hurricane wrack unrolls up the front of the sky,

At once the ship lies idle, the sails hang silent on high,

The breath of the wind that blew is blown out like the flame of a lamp,

And the silent armies of death draw near with inaudible tramp:

So sudden, the voice of her weeping ceased; in silence she rose

And passed from the house of her sorrow, a woman clothed with repose,

Carrying death in her breast and sharpening death with her hand.

Hither she went and thither in all the coasts of the land.

They tell that she feared not to slumber alone, in the dead of night,

In accursed places; beheld, unblenched, the ribbon of light [21]

Spin from temple to temple; guided the perilous skiff,

Abhorred not the paths of the mountain and trod the verge of the cliff;

From end to end of the island, thought not the distance long,

But forth from king to king carried the tale of her wrong.

To king after king, as they sat in the palace door, she came,

Claiming kinship, declaiming verses, naming her name

And the names of all of her fathers; and still, with a heart on the rack,

Jested to capture a hearing and laughed when they jested back:

So would deceive them awhile, and change and return in a breath,

And on all the men of Vaiau imprecate instant death;

And tempt her kings—for Vaiau was a rich and prosperous land,

And flatter—for who would attempt it but warriors mighty of hand?

And change in a breath again and rise in a strain of song,

Invoking the beaten drums, beholding the fall of the strong,

Calling the fowls of the air to come and feast on the dead.

And they held the chin in silence, and heard her, and shook the head;

For they knew the men of Taiárapu famous in battle and feast,

Marvellous eaters and smiters: the men of Vaiau not least.

To the land of the Námunu-úra, [23a] to Paea, at length she came,

To men who were foes to the Tevas and hated their race and name.

There was she well received, and spoke with Hiopa the king. [23b]

And Hiopa listened, and weighed, and wisely considered the thing.

"Here in the back of the isle we dwell in a sheltered place,"

Quoth he to the woman, "in quiet, a weak and peaceable race.

But far in the teeth of the wind lofty Taiárapu lies;

Strong blows the wind of the trade on its seaward face, and cries

Aloud in the top of arduous mountains, and utters its song

In green continuous forests. Strong is the wind, and strong

And fruitful and hardy the race, famous in battle and feast,

Marvellous eaters and smiters: the men of Vaiau not least.

Now hearken to me, my daughter, and hear a word of the wise:

How a strength goes linked with a weakness, two by two, like the eyes.

They can wield the ómare well and cast the javelin far;

Yet are they greedy and weak as the swine and the children are.

Plant we, then, here at Paea, a garden of excellent fruits;

Plant we bananas and kava and taro, the king of roots;

Let the pigs in Paea be tapu [25] and no man fish for a year;

And of all the meat in Tahiti gather we threefold here.

So shall the fame of our plenty fill the island, and so,

At last, on the tongue of rumour, go where we wish it to go.

Then shall the pigs of Taiárapu raise their snouts in the air;

But we sit quiet and wait, as the fowler sits by the snare,

And tranquilly fold our hands, till the pigs come nosing the food:

But meanwhile build us a house of Trotéa, the stubborn wood,

Bind it with incombustible thongs, set a roof to the room,

Too strong for the hands of a man to dissever or fire to consume;

And there, when the pigs come trotting, there shall the feast be spread,

There shall the eye of the morn enlighten the feasters dead.

So be it done; for I have a heart that pities your state,

And Nateva and Námunu-úra are fire and water for hate."

All was done as he said, and the gardens prospered; and now

The fame of their plenty went out, and word of it came to Vaiau.

For the men of Námunu-úra sailed, to the windward far,

Lay in the offing by south where the towns of the Tevas are,

And cast overboard of their plenty; and lo! at the Tevas feet

The surf on all of the beaches tumbled treasures of meat.

In the salt of the sea, a harvest tossed with the refluent foam;

And the children gleaned it in playing, and ate and carried it home;

And the elders stared and debated, and wondered and passed the jest,

But whenever a guest came by eagerly questioned the guest;

And little by little, from one to another, the word went round:

"In all the borders of Paea the victual rots on the ground,

And swine are plenty as rats. And now, when they fare to the sea,

The men of the Námunu-úra glean from under the tree

And load the canoe to the gunwale with all that is toothsome to eat;

And all day long on the sea the jaws are crushing the meat,

The steersman eats at the helm, the rowers munch at the oar,

And at length, when their bellies are full, overboard with the store!"

Now was the word made true, and soon as the bait was bare,

All the pigs of Taiárapu raised their snouts in the air.

Songs were recited, and kinship was counted, and tales were told

How war had severed of late but peace had cemented of old

The clans of the island. "To war," said they, "now set we an end,

And hie to the Námunu-úra even as a friend to a friend."

So judged, and a day was named; and soon as the morning broke,

Canoes were thrust in the sea and the houses emptied of folk.

Strong blew the wind of the south, the wind that gathers the clan;

Along all the line of the reef the clamorous surges ran;

And the clouds were piled on the top of the island mountain-high,

A mountain throned on a mountain. The fleet of canoes swept by

In the midst, on the green lagoon, with a crew released from care,

Sailing an even water, breathing a summer air,

Cheered by a cloudless sun; and ever to left and right,

Bursting surge on the reef, drenching storms on the height.

So the folk of Vaiau sailed and were glad all day,

Coasting the palm-tree cape and crossing the populous bay

By all the towns of the Tevas; and still as they bowled along,

Boat would answer to boat with jest and laughter and song,

And the people of all the towns trooped to the sides of the sea

And gazed from under the hand or sprang aloft on the tree,

Hailing and cheering. Time failed them for more to do;

The holiday village careened to the wind, and was gone from view

Swift as a passing bird; and ever as onward it bore,

Like the cry of the passing bird, bequeathed its song to the shore—

Desirable laughter of maids and the cry of delight of the child.

And the gazer, left behind, stared at the wake and smiled.

By all the towns of the Tevas they went, and Pápara last,

The home of the chief, the place of muster in war; and passed

The march of the lands of the clan, to the lands of an alien folk.

And there, from the dusk of the shoreside palms, a column of smoke

Mounted and wavered and died in the gold of the setting sun,

"Paea!" they cried. "It is Paea." And so was the voyage done.

In the early fall of the night, Hiopa came to the shore,

And beheld and counted the comers, and lo, they were forty score:

The pelting feet of the babes that ran already and played,

The clean-lipped smile of the boy, the slender breasts of the maid,

And mighty limbs of women, stalwart mothers of men.

The sires stood forth unabashed; but a little back from his ken

Clustered the scarcely nubile, the lads and maids, in a ring,

Fain of each other, afraid of themselves, aware of the king

And aping behaviour, but clinging together with hands and eyes,

With looks that were kind like kisses, and laughter tender as sighs.

There, too, the grandsire stood, raising his silver crest,

And the impotent hands of a suckling groped in his barren breast.

The childhood of love, the pair well married, the innocent brood,

The tale of the generations repeated and ever renewed—

Hiopa beheld them together, all the ages of man,

And a moment shook in his purpose.

But these were the foes of his clan,

And he trod upon pity, and came, and civilly greeted the king,

And gravely entreated Rahéro; and for all that could fight or sing,

And claimed a name in the land, had fitting phrases of praise;

But with all who were well-descended he spoke of the ancient days.

And "'Tis true," said he, "that in Paea the victual rots on the ground;

But, friends, your number is many; and pigs must be hunted and found,

And the lads troop to the mountains to bring the féis down,

And around the bowls of the kava cluster the maids of the town.

So, for to-night, sleep here; but king, common, and priest

To-morrow, in order due, shall sit with me in the feast."

Sleepless the live-long night, Hiopa's followers toiled.

The pigs screamed and were slaughtered; the spars of the guest-house oiled,

The leaves spread on the floor. In many a mountain glen

The moon drew shadows of trees on the naked bodies of men

Plucking and bearing fruits; and in all the bounds of the town

Red glowed the cocoanut fires, and were buried and trodden down.

Thus did seven of the yottowas toil with their tale of the clan,

But the eighth wrought with his lads, hid from the sight of man.

In the deeps of the woods they laboured, piling the fuel high

In fagots, the load of a man, fuel seasoned and dry,

Thirsty to seize upon fire and apt to blurt into flame.

And now was the day of the feast. The forests, as morning came,

Tossed in the wind, and the peaks quaked in the blaze of the day

And the cocoanuts showered on the ground, rebounding and rolling away:

A glorious morn for a feast, a famous wind for a fire.

To the hall of feasting Hiopa led them, mother and sire

And maid and babe in a tale, the whole of the holiday throng.

Smiling they came, garlanded green, not dreaming of wrong;

And for every three, a pig, tenderly cooked in the ground,

Waited, and féi, the staff of life, heaped in a mound

For each where he sat;—for each, bananas roasted and raw

Piled with a bountiful hand, as for horses hay and straw

Are stacked in a stable; and fish, the food of desire, [34]

And plentiful vessels of sauce, and breadfruit gilt in the fire;—

And kava was common as water. Feasts have there been ere now,

And many, but never a feast like that of the folk of Vaiau.

All day long they ate with the resolute greed of brutes,

And turned from the pigs to the fish, and again from the fish to the fruits,

And emptied the vessels of sauce, and drank of the kava deep;

Till the young lay stupid as stones, and the strongest nodded to sleep.

Sleep that was mighty as death and blind as a moonless night

Tethered them hand and foot; and their souls were drowned, and the light

Was cloaked from their eyes. Senseless together, the old and the young,

The fighter deadly to smite and the prater cunning of tongue,

The woman wedded and fruitful, inured to the pangs of birth,

And the maid that knew not of kisses, blindly sprawled on the earth.

From the hall Hiopa the king and his chiefs came stealthily forth.

Already the sun hung low and enlightened the peaks of the north;

But the wind was stubborn to die and blew as it blows at morn,

Showering the nuts in the dusk, and e'en as a banner is torn,

High on the peaks of the island, shattered the mountain cloud.

And now at once, at a signal, a silent, emulous crowd

Set hands to the work of death, hurrying to and fro,

Like ants, to furnish the fagots, building them broad and low,

And piling them high and higher around the walls of the hall.

Silence persisted within, for sleep lay heavy on all;

But the mother of Támatéa stood at Hiopa's side,

And shook for terror and joy like a girl that is a bride.

Night fell on the toilers, and first Hiopa the wise

Made the round of the house, visiting all with his eyes;

And all was piled to the eaves, and fuel blockaded the door;

And within, in the house beleaguered, slumbered the forty score.

Then was an aito dispatched and came with fire in his hand,

And Hiopa took it.—"Within," said he, "is the life of a land;

And behold! I breathe on the coal, I breathe on the dales of the east,

And silence falls on forest and shore; the voice of the feast

Is quenched, and the smoke of cooking; the rooftree decays and falls

On the empty lodge, and the winds subvert deserted walls."

Therewithal, to the fuel, he laid the glowing coal;

And the redness ran in the mass and burrowed within like a mole,

And copious smoke was conceived. But, as when a dam is to burst,

The water lips it and crosses in silver trickles at first,

And then, of a sudden, whelms and bears it away forthright:

So now, in a moment, the flame sprang and towered in the night,

And wrestled and roared in the wind, and high over house and tree,

Stood, like a streaming torch, enlightening land and sea.

But the mother of Támatéa threw her arms abroad,

"Pyre of my son," she shouted, "debited vengeance of God,

Late, late, I behold you, yet I behold you at last,

And glory, beholding! For now are the days of my agony past,

The lust that famished my soul now eats and drinks its desire,

And they that encompassed my son shrivel alive in the fire.

Tenfold precious the vengeance that comes after lingering years!

Ye quenched the voice of my singer?—hark, in your dying ears,

The song of the conflagration! Ye left me a widow alone?

—Behold, the whole of your race consumes, sinew and bone

And torturing flesh together: man, mother, and maid

Heaped in a common shambles; and already, borne by the trade,

The smoke of your dissolution darkens the stars of night."

Thus she spoke, and her stature grew in the people's sight.

III. RAHÉRO

Rahéro was there in the hall asleep: beside him his wife,

Comely, a mirthful woman, one that delighted in life;

And a girl that was ripe for marriage, shy and sly as a mouse;

And a boy, a climber of trees: all the hopes of his house.

Unwary, with open hands, he slept in the midst of his folk,

And dreamed that he heard a voice crying without, and awoke,

Leaping blindly afoot like one from a dream that he fears.

A hellish glow and clouds were about him;—it roared in his ears

Like the sound of the cataract fall that plunges sudden and steep;

And Rahéro swayed as he stood, and his reason was still asleep.

Now the flame struck hard on the house, wind-wielded, a fracturing blow,

And the end of the roof was burst and fell on the sleepers below;

And the lofty hall, and the feast, and the prostrate bodies of folk,

Shone red in his eyes a moment, and then were swallowed of smoke.

In the mind of Rahéro clearness came; and he opened his throat;

And as when a squall comes sudden, the straining sail of a boat

Thunders aloud and bursts, so thundered the voice of the man.

—"The wind and the rain!" he shouted, the mustering word of the clan, [41]

And "up!" and "to arms men of Vaiau!" But silence replied,

Or only the voice of the gusts of the fire, and nothing beside.

Rahéro stooped and groped. He handled his womankind,

But the fumes of the fire and the kava had quenched the life of their mind,

And they lay like pillars prone; and his hand encountered the boy,

And there sprang in the gloom of his soul a sudden lightning of joy.

"Him can I save!" he thought, "if I were speedy enough."

And he loosened the cloth from his loins, and swaddled the child in the stuff;

And about the strength of his neck he knotted the burden well.

There where the roof had fallen, it roared like the mouth of hell.

Thither Rahéro went, stumbling on senseless folk,

And grappled a post of the house, and began to climb in the smoke:

The last alive of Vaiau; and the son borne by the sire.

The post glowed in the grain with ulcers of eating fire,

And the fire bit to the blood and mangled his hands and thighs;

And the fumes sang in his head like wine and stung in his eyes;

And still he climbed, and came to the top, the place of proof,

And thrust a hand through the flame, and clambered alive on the roof.

But even as he did so, the wind, in a garment of flames and pain,

Wrapped him from head to heel; and the waistcloth parted in twain;

And the living fruit of his loins dropped in the fire below.

About the blazing feast-house clustered the eyes of the foe,

Watching, hand upon weapon, lest ever a soul should flee,

Shading the brow from the glare, straining the neck to see

Only, to leeward, the flames in the wind swept far and wide,

And the forest sputtered on fire; and there might no man abide.

Thither Rahéro crept, and dropped from the burning eaves,

And crouching low to the ground, in a treble covert of leaves

And fire and volleying smoke, ran for the life of his soul

Unseen; and behind him under a furnace of ardent coal,

Cairned with a wonder of flame, and blotting the night with smoke,

Blazed and were smelted together the bones of all his folk.

He fled unguided at first; but hearing the breakers roar,

Thitherward shaped his way, and came at length to the shore.

Sound-limbed he was: dry-eyed; but smarted in every part;

And the mighty cage of his ribs heaved on his straining heart

With sorrow and rage. And "Fools!" he cried, "fools of Vaiau,

Heads of swine—gluttons—Alas! and where are they now?

Those that I played with, those that nursed me, those that I nursed?

God, and I outliving them! I, the least and the worst—

I, that thought myself crafty, snared by this herd of swine,

In the tortures of hell and desolate, stripped of all that was mine:

All!—my friends and my fathers—the silver heads of yore

That trooped to the council, the children that ran to the open door

Crying with innocent voices and clasping a father's knees!

And mine, my wife—my daughter—my sturdy climber of trees

Ah, never to climb again!"

Thus in the dusk of the night,

(For clouds rolled in the sky and the moon was swallowed from sight,)

Pacing and gnawing his fists, Rahéro raged by the shore.

Vengeance: that must be his. But much was to do before;

And first a single life to be snatched from a deadly place,

A life, the root of revenge, surviving plant of the race:

And next the race to be raised anew, and the lands of the clan

Repeopled. So Rahéro designed, a prudent man

Even in wrath, and turned for the means of revenge and escape:

A boat to be seized by stealth, a wife to be taken by rape.

Still was the dark lagoon; beyond on the coral wall,

He saw the breakers shine, he heard them bellow and fall.

Alone, on the top of the reef, a man with a flaming brand

Walked, gazing and pausing, a fish-spear poised in his hand.

The foam boiled to his calf when the mightier breakers came,

And the torch shed in the wind scattering tufts of flame.

Afar on the dark lagoon a canoe lay idly at wait:

A figure dimly guiding it: surely the fisherman's mate.

Rahéro saw and he smiled. He straightened his mighty thews:

Naked, with never a weapon, and covered with scorch and bruise,

He straightened his arms, he filled the void of his body with breath,

And, strong as the wind in his manhood, doomed the fisher to death.

Silent he entered the water, and silently swam, and came

There where the fisher walked, holding on high the flame.

Loud on the pier of the reef volleyed the breach of the sea;

And hard at the back of the man, Rahéro crept to his knee

On the coral, and suddenly sprang and seized him, the elder hand

Clutching the joint of his throat, the other snatching the brand

Ere it had time to fall, and holding it steady and high.

Strong was the fisher, brave, and swift of mind and of eye—

Strongly he threw in the clutch; but Rahéro resisted the strain,

And jerked, and the spine of life snapped with a crack in twain,

And the man came slack in his hands and tumbled a lump at his feet.

One moment: and there, on the reef, where the breakers whitened and beat,

Rahéro was standing alone, glowing and scorched and bare,

A victor unknown of any, raising the torch in the air.

But once he drank of his breath, and instantly set him to fish

Like a man intent upon supper at home and a savoury dish.

For what should the woman have seen? A man with a torch—and then

A moment's blur of the eyes—and a man with a torch again.

And the torch had scarcely been shaken. "Ah, surely," Rahéro said,

"She will deem it a trick of the eyes, a fancy born in the head;

But time must be given the fool to nourish a fool's belief."

So for a while, a sedulous fisher, he walked the reef,

Pausing at times and gazing, striking at times with the spear:

—Lastly, uttered the call; and even as the boat drew near,

Like a man that was done with its use, tossed the torch in the sea.

Lightly he leaped on the boat beside the woman; and she

Lightly addressed him, and yielded the paddle and place to sit;

For now the torch was extinguished the night was black as the pit

Rahéro set him to row, never a word he spoke,

And the boat sang in the water urged by his vigorous stroke.

—"What ails you?" the woman asked, "and why did you drop the brand?

We have only to kindle another as soon as we come to land."

Never a word Rahéro replied, but urged the canoe.

And a chill fell on the woman.—"Atta! speak! is it you?

Speak! Why are you silent? Why do you bend aside?

Wherefore steer to the seaward?" thus she panted and cried.

Never a word from the oarsman, toiling there in the dark;

But right for a gate of the reef he silently headed the bark,

And wielding the single paddle with passionate sweep on sweep,

Drove her, the little fitted, forth on the open deep.

And fear, there where she sat, froze the woman to stone:

Not fear of the crazy boat and the weltering deep alone;

But a keener fear of the night, the dark, and the ghostly hour,

And the thing that drove the canoe with more than a mortal's power

And more than a mortal's boldness. For much she knew of the dead

That haunt and fish upon reefs, toiling, like men, for bread,

And traffic with human fishers, or slay them and take their ware,

Till the hour when the star of the dead [51a] goes down, and the morning air

Blows, and the cocks are singing on shore. And surely she knew

The speechless thing at her side belonged to the grave. [51b]

It blew

All night from the south; all night, Rahéro contended and kept

The prow to the cresting sea; and, silent as though she slept,

The woman huddled and quaked. And now was the peep of day.

High and long on their left the mountainous island lay;

And over the peaks of Taiárapu arrows of sunlight struck.

On shore the birds were beginning to sing: the ghostly ruck

Of the buried had long ago returned to the covered grave;

And here on the sea, the woman, waxing suddenly brave,

Turned her swiftly about and looked in the face of the man.

And sure he was none that she knew, none of her country or clan:

A stranger, mother-naked, and marred with the marks of fire,

But comely and great of stature, a man to obey and admire.

And Rahéro regarded her also, fixed, with a frowning face,

Judging the woman's fitness to mother a warlike race.

Broad of shoulder, ample of girdle, long in the thigh,

Deep of bosom she was, and bravely supported his eye.

"Woman," said he, "last night the men of your folk—

Man, woman, and maid, smothered my race in smoke.

It was done like cowards; and I, a mighty man of my hands,

Escaped, a single life; and now to the empty lands

And smokeless hearths of my people, sail, with yourself, alone.

Before your mother was born, the die of to-day was thrown

And you selected:—your husband, vainly striving, to fall

Broken between these hands:—yourself to be severed from all,

The places, the people, you love—home, kindred, and clan—

And to dwell in a desert and bear the babes of a kinless man."

NOTES TO THE SONG OF RAHÉRO

Introduction.—This tale, of which I have not consciously changed a single feature, I received from tradition. It is highly popular through all the country of the eight Tevas, the clan to which Rahéro belonged; and particularly in Taiárapu, the windward peninsula of Tahiti, where he lived. I have heard from end to end two versions; and as many as five different persons have helped me with details. There seems no reason why the tale should not be true.

[5] Note 1. "The aito," quasi champion, or brave. One skilled in the use of some weapon, who wandered the country challenging distinguished rivals and taking part in local quarrels. It was in the natural course of his advancement to be at last employed by a chief, or king; and it would then be a part of his duties to purvey the victim for sacrifice. One of the doomed families was indicated; the aito took his weapon and went forth alone; a little behind him bearers followed with the sacrificial basket. Sometimes the victim showed fight, sometimes prevailed; more often, without doubt, he fell. But whatever body was found, the bearers indifferently took up.

[7] Note 2. "Pai," "Honoura," and "Ahupu." Legendary persons of Tahiti, all natives of Taiárapu. Of the first two, I have collected singular although imperfect legends, which I hope soon to lay before the public in another place. Of Ahupu, except in snatches of song, little memory appears to linger. She dwelt at least about Tepari,—"the sea-cliffs,"—the eastern fastness of the isle; walked by paths known only to herself upon the mountains; was courted by dangerous suitors who came swimming from adjacent islands, and defended and rescued (as I gather) by the loyalty of native fish. My anxiety to learn more of "Ahupu Vehine" became (during my stay in Taiárapu) a cause of some diversion to that mirthful people, the inhabitants.

[10a] Note 3. "Covered an oven." The cooking fire is made in a hole in the ground, and is then buried.

[10b] Note 4. "Flies." This is perhaps an anachronism. Even speaking

of to-day in Tahiti, the phrase would have to be understood as referring mainly to mosquitoes, and these only in watered valleys with close woods, such as I suppose to form the surroundings of Rahéro's homestead. Quarter of a mile away, where the air moves freely, you shall look in vain for one.

[13] Note 5. "Hook" of mother-of-pearl. Bright-hook fishing, and that with the spear, appear to be the favourite native methods.

[14] Note 6. "Leaves," the plates of Tahiti.

[16] Note 7. "Yottowas," so spelt for convenience of pronunciation, quasi Tacksmen in the Scottish Highlands. The organisation of eight subdistricts and eight yottowas to a division, which was in use (until yesterday) among the Tevas, I have attributed without authority to the next clan: see page 33.

[17] Note 8. "Omare," pronounce as a dactyl. A loaded quarter-staff, one of the two favourite weapons of the Tahitian brave; the javelin, or casting spear, was the other.

[21] Note 9. "The ribbon of light." Still to be seen (and heard) spinning from one marae to another on Tahiti; or so I have it upon evidence that would rejoice the Psychical Society.

[23a] Note 10. "Námunu-úra." The complete name is Namunu-ura te aropa. Why it should be pronounced Námunu, dactyllically, I cannot see, but so I have always heard it. This was the clan immediately beyond the Tevas on the south coast of the island. At the date of the tale the clan organisation must have been very weak. There is no particular mention of Támatéa's mother going to Papara, to the head chief of her own clan, which would appear her natural recourse. On the other hand, she seems to have visited various lesser chiefs among the Tevas, and these to have excused themselves solely on the danger of the enterprise. The broad distinction here drawn between Nateva and Námunu-úra is therefore not impossibly anachronistic.

[23b] Note 11. "Hiopa the king." Hiopa was really the name of the king (chief) of Vaiau; but I could never learn that of the king of Paea—pronounce to rhyme with the Indian ayah—and I gave the name where it was most needed. This note must appear otiose indeed to readers who have never

heard of either of these two gentlemen; and perhaps there is only one person in the world capable at once of reading my verses and spying the inaccuracy. For him, for Mr. Tati Salmon, hereditary high chief of the Tevas, the note is solely written: a small attention from a clansman to his chief.

[25] Note 12. "Let the pigs be tapu." It is impossible to explain tapu in a note; we have it as an English word, taboo. Suffice it, that a thing which was tapu must not be touched, nor a place that was tapu visited.

[34] Note 13. "Fish, the food of desire." There is a special word in the Tahitian language to signify hungering after fish. I may remark that here is one of my chief difficulties about the whole story. How did king, commons, women, and all come to eat together at this feast? But it troubled none of my numerous authorities; so there must certainly be some natural explanation.

[41] Note 14. "The mustering word of the clan."

Teva te ua,

Teva te matai!

Teva the wind,

Teva the rain!

[51a] Note 15. "The star of the dead." Venus as a morning star. I have collected much curious evidence as to this belief. The dead retain their taste for a fish diet, enter into copartnery with living fishers, and haunt the reef and the lagoon. The conclusion attributed to the nameless lady of the legend would be reached to-day, under the like circumstances, by ninety per cent of Polynesians: and here I probably understate by one-tenth.

[51b] Note 16. See note 15 above.

THE FEAST OF FAMINE: MARQUESAN MANNERS

I. THE PRIEST'S VIGIL

In all the land of the tribe was neither fish nor fruit,

And the deepest pit of popoi stood empty to the foot. [61]

The clans upon the left and the clans upon the right

Now oiled their carven maces and scoured their daggers bright;

They gat them to the thicket, to the deepest of the shade,

And lay with sleepless eyes in the deadly ambuscade.

And oft in the starry even the song of morning rose,

What time the oven smoked in the country of their foes;

For oft to loving hearts, and waiting ears and sight,

The lads that went to forage returned not with the night.

Now first the children sickened, and then the women paled,

And the great arms of the warrior no more for war availed.

Hushed was the deep drum, discarded was the dance;

And those that met the priest now glanced at him askance.

The priest was a man of years, his eyes were ruby-red, [62a]

He neither feared the dark nor the terrors of the dead,

He knew the songs of races, the names of ancient date;

And the beard upon his bosom would have bought the chief's estate.

He dwelt in a high-built lodge, hard by the roaring shore,

Raised on a noble terrace and with tikis [62b] at the door.

Within it was full of riches, for he served his nation well,

And full of the sound of breakers, like the hollow of a shell.

For weeks he let them perish, gave never a helping sign,

But sat on his oiled platform to commune with the divine,

But sat on his high terrace, with the tikis by his side,

And stared on the blue ocean, like a parrot, ruby-eyed.

Dawn as yellow as sulphur leaped on the mountain height:

Out on the round of the sea the gems of the morning light,

Up from the round of the sea the streamers of the sun;—

But down in the depths of the valley the day was not begun.

In the blue of the woody twilight burned red the cocoa-husk,

And the women and men of the clan went forth to bathe in the dusk,

A word that began to go round, a word, a whisper, a start:

Hope that leaped in the bosom, fear that knocked on the heart:

"See, the priest is not risen—look, for his door is fast!

He is going to name the victims; he is going to help us at last."

Thrice rose the sun to noon; and ever, like one of the dead,

The priest lay still in his house with the roar of the sea in his head;

There was never a foot on the floor, there was never a whisper of speech;

Only the leering tikis stared on the blinding beach.

Again were the mountains fired, again the morning broke;

And all the houses lay still, but the house of the priest awoke.

Close in their covering roofs lay and trembled the clan,

But the agèd, red-eyed priest ran forth like a lunatic man;

And the village panted to see him in the jewels of death again,

In the silver beards of the old and the hair of women slain.

Frenzy shook in his limbs, frenzy shone in his eyes,

And still and again as he ran, the valley rang with his cries.

All day long in the land, by cliff and thicket and den,

He ran his lunatic rounds, and howled for the flesh of men;

All day long he ate not, nor ever drank of the brook;

And all day long in their houses the people listened and shook—

All day long in their houses they listened with bated breath,

And never a soul went forth, for the sight of the priest was death.

Three were the days of his running, as the gods appointed of yore,

Two the nights of his sleeping alone in the place of gore:

The drunken slumber of frenzy twice he drank to the lees,

On the sacred stones of the High-place under the sacred trees;

With a lamp at his ashen head he lay in the place of the feast,

And the sacred leaves of the banyan rustled around the priest.

Last, when the stated even fell upon terrace and tree,

And the shade of the lofty island lay leagues away to sea,

And all the valleys of verdure were heavy with manna and musk,

The wreck of the red-eyed priest came gasping home in the dusk.

He reeled across the village, he staggered along the shore,

And between the leering tikis crept groping through his door.

There went a stir through the lodges, the voice of speech awoke;

Once more from the builded platforms arose the evening smoke.

And those who were mighty in war, and those renowned for an art

Sat in their stated seats and talked of the morrow apart.

II. THE LOVERS

Hark! away in the woods—for the ears of love are sharp—

Stealthily, quietly touched, the note of the one-stringed harp. [67]

In the lighted house of her father, why should Taheia start?

Taheia heavy of hair, Taheia tender of heart,

Taheia the well-descended, a bountiful dealer in love,

Nimble of foot like the deer, and kind of eye like the dove?

Sly and shy as a cat, with never a change of face,

Taheia slips to the door, like one that would breathe a space;

Saunters and pauses, and looks at the stars, and lists to the seas;

Then sudden and swift as a cat, she plunges under the trees.

Swift as a cat she runs, with her garment gathered high,

Leaping, nimble of foot, running, certain of eye;

And ever to guide her way over the smooth and the sharp,

Ever nearer and nearer the note of the one-stringed harp;

Till at length, in a glade of the wood, with a naked mountain above,

The sound of the harp thrown down, and she in the arms of her love.

"Rua,"—"Taheia," they cry—"my heart, my soul, and my eyes,"

And clasp and sunder and kiss, with lovely laughter and sighs,

"Rua!"—"Taheia, my love,"—"Rua, star of my night,

Clasp me, hold me, and love me, single spring of delight."

And Rua folded her close, he folded her near and long,

The living knit to the living, and sang the lover's song:

Night, night it is, night upon the palms.

Night, night it is, the land wind has blown.

Starry, starry night, over deep and height;

Love, love in the valley, love all alone.

"Taheia, heavy of hair, a foolish thing have we done,

To bind what gods have sundered unkindly into one.

Why should a lowly lover have touched Taheia's skirt,

Taheia the well-descended, and Rua child of the dirt?"

"—On high with the haka-ikis my father sits in state,

Ten times fifty kinsmen salute him in the gate;

Round all his martial body, and in bands across his face,

The marks of the tattooer proclaim his lofty place.

I too, in the hands of the cunning, in the sacred cabin of palm, [69]

Have shrunk like the mimosa, and bleated like the lamb;

Round half my tender body, that none shall clasp but you,

For a crest and a fair adornment go dainty lines of blue.

Love, love, beloved Rua, love levels all degrees,

And the well-tattooed Taheia clings panting to your knees."

"—Taheia, song of the morning, how long is the longest love?

A cry, a clasp of the hands, a star that falls from above!

Ever at morn in the blue, and at night when all is black,

Ever it skulks and trembles with the hunter, Death, on its track.

Hear me, Taheia, death! For to-morrow the priest shall awake,

And the names be named of the victims to bleed for the nation's sake;

And first of the numbered many that shall be slain ere noon,

Rua the child of the dirt, Rua the kinless loon.

For him shall the drum be beat, for him be raised the song,

For him to the sacred High-place the chaunting people throng,

For him the oven smoke as for a speechless beast,

And the sire of my Taheia come greedy to the feast."

"Rua, be silent, spare me. Taheia closes her ears.

Pity my yearning heart, pity my girlish years!

Flee from the cruel hands, flee from the knife and coal,

Lie hid in the deeps of the woods, Rua, sire of my soul!"

"Whither to flee, Taheia, whither in all of the land?

The fires of the bloody kitchen are kindled on every hand;

On every hand in the isle a hungry whetting of teeth,

Eyes in the trees above, arms in the brush beneath.

Patience to lie in wait, cunning to follow the sleuth,

Abroad the foes I have fought, and at home the friends of my youth."

"Love, love, beloved Rua, love has a clearer eye,

Hence from the arms of love you go not forth to die.

There, where the broken mountain drops sheer into the glen,

There shall you find a hold from the boldest hunter of men;

There, in the deep recess, where the sun falls only at noon,

And only once in the night enters the light of the moon,

Nor ever a sound but of birds, or the rain when it falls with a shout;

For death and the fear of death beleaguer the valley about.

Tapu it is, but the gods will surely pardon despair;

Tapu, but what of that? If Rua can only dare.

Tapu and tapu and tapu, I know they are every one right;

But the god of every tapu is not always quick to smite.

Lie secret there, my Rua, in the arms of awful gods,

Sleep in the shade of the trees on the couch of the kindly sods,

Sleep and dream of Taheia, Taheia will wake for you;

And whenever the land wind blows and the woods are heavy with dew,

Alone through the horror of night, [72] with food for the soul of her love,

Taheia the undissuaded will hurry true as the dove."

"Taheia, the pit of the night crawls with treacherous things,

Spirits of ultimate air and the evil souls of things;

The souls of the dead, the stranglers, that perch in the trees of the wood,

Waiters for all things human, haters of evil and good."

"Rua, behold me, kiss me, look in my eyes and read;

Are these the eyes of a maid that would leave her lover in need?

Brave in the eye of day, my father ruled in the fight;

The child of his loins, Taheia, will play the man in the night."

So it was spoken, and so agreed, and Taheia arose

And smiled in the stars and was gone, swift as the swallow goes;

And Rua stood on the hill, and sighed, and followed her flight,

And there were the lodges below, each with its door alight;

From folk that sat on the terrace and drew out the even long

Sudden crowings of laughter, monotonous drone of song;

The quiet passage of souls over his head in the trees; [74]

And from all around the haven the crumbling thunder of seas.

"Farewell, my home," said Rua. "Farewell, O quiet seat!

To-morrow in all your valleys the drum of death shall beat."

III. THE FEAST

Dawn as yellow as sulphur leaped on the naked peak,

And all the village was stirring, for now was the priest to speak.

Forth on his terrace he came, and sat with the chief in talk;

His lips were blackened with fever, his cheeks were whiter than chalk;

Fever clutched at his hands, fever nodded his head,

But, quiet and steady and cruel, his eyes shone ruby-red.

In the earliest rays of the sun the chief rose up content;

Braves were summoned, and drummers; messengers came and went;

Braves ran to their lodges, weapons were snatched from the wall;

The commons herded together, and fear was over them all.

Festival dresses they wore, but the tongue was dry in their mouth,

And the blinking eyes in their faces skirted from north to south.

Now to the sacred enclosure gathered the greatest and least,

And from under the shade of the banyan arose the voice of the feast,

The frenzied roll of the drum, and a swift, monotonous song.

Higher the sun swam up; the trade wind level and strong

Awoke in the tops of the palms and rattled the fans aloud,

And over the garlanded heads and shining robes of the crowd

Tossed the spiders of shadow, scattered the jewels of sun.

Forty the tale of the drums, and the forty throbbed like one;

A thousand hearts in the crowd, and the even chorus of song,

Swift as the feet of a runner, trampled a thousand strong.

And the old men leered at the ovens and licked their lips for the food;

And the women stared at the lads, and laughed and looked to the wood.

As when the sweltering baker, at night, when the city is dead,

Alone in the trough of labour treads and fashions the bread;

So in the heat, and the reek, and the touch of woman and man,

The naked spirit of evil kneaded the hearts of the clan.

Now cold was at many a heart, and shaking in many a seat;

For there were the empty baskets, but who was to furnish the meat?

For here was the nation assembled, and there were the ovens anigh,

And out of a thousand singers nine were numbered to die.

Till, of a sudden, a shock, a mace in the air, a yell,

And, struck in the edge of the crowd, the first of the victims fell. [78]

Terror and horrible glee divided the shrinking clan,

Terror of what was to follow, glee for a diet of man.

Frenzy hurried the chaunt, frenzy rattled the drums;

The nobles, high on the terrace, greedily mouthed their thumbs;

And once and again and again, in the ignorant crowd below,

Once and again and again descended the murderous blow.

Now smoked the oven, and now, with the cutting lip of a shell,

A butcher of ninety winters jointed the bodies well.

Unto the carven lodge, silent, in order due,

The grandees of the nation one after one withdrew;

And a line of laden bearers brought to the terrace foot,

On poles across their shoulders, the last reserve of fruit.

The victims bled for the nobles in the old appointed way;

The fruit was spread for the commons, for all should eat to-day.

And now was the kava brewed, and now the cocoa ran,

Now was the hour of the dance for child and woman and man;

And mirth was in every heart, and a garland on every head,

And all was well with the living and well with the eight who were dead.

Only the chiefs and the priest talked and consulted awhile:

"To-morrow," they said, and "To-morrow," and nodded and seemed to smile:

"Rua the child of dirt, the creature of common clay,

Rua must die to-morrow, since Rua is gone to-day."

Out of the groves of the valley, where clear the blackbirds sang.

Sheer from the trees of the valley the face of the mountain sprang;

Sheer and bare it rose, unscalable barricade,

Beaten and blown against by the generous draught of the trade.

Dawn on its fluted brow painted rainbow light,

Close on its pinnacled crown trembled the stars at night.

Here and there in a cleft clustered contorted trees,

Or the silver beard of a stream hung and swung in the breeze.

High overhead, with a cry, the torrents leaped for the main,

And silently sprinkled below in thin perennial rain.

Dark in the staring noon, dark was Rua's ravine,

Damp and cold was the air, and the face of the cliffs was green.

Here, in the rocky pit, accursed already of old,

On a stone in the midst of a river, Rua sat and was cold.

"Valley of mid-day shadows, valley of silent falls,"

Rua sang, and his voice went hollow about the walls,

"Valley of shadow and rock, a doleful prison to me,

What is the life you can give to a child of the sun and the sea?"

And Rua arose and came to the open mouth of the glen,

Whence he beheld the woods, and the sea, and houses of men.

Wide blew the riotous trade, and smelt in his nostrils good;

It bowed the boats on the bay, and tore and divided the wood;

It smote and sundered the groves as Moses smote with the rod,

And the streamers of all the trees blew like banners abroad;

And ever and on, in a lull, the trade wind brought him along

A far-off patter of drums and a far-off whisper of song.

Swift as the swallow's wings, the diligent hands on the drum

Fluttered and hurried and throbbed. "Ah, woe that I hear you come,"

Rua cried in his grief, "a sorrowful sound to me,

Mounting far and faint from the resonant shore of the sea!

Woe in the song! for the grave breathes in the singers' breath,

And I hear in the tramp of the drums the beat of the heart of death.

Home of my youth! no more, through all the length of the years,

No more to the place of the echoes of early laughter and tears,

No more shall Rua return; no more as the evening ends,

To crowded eyes of welcome, to the reaching hands of friends."

All day long from the High-place the drums and the singing came,

And the even fell, and the sun went down, a wheel of flame;

And night came gleaning the shadows and hushing the sounds of the wood;

And silence slept on all, where Rua sorrowed and stood.

But still from the shore of the bay the sound of the festival rang,

And still the crowd in the High-place danced and shouted and sang.

Now over all the isle terror was breathed abroad

Of shadowy hands from the trees and shadowy snares in the sod;

And before the nostrils of night, the shuddering hunter of men

Hurried, with beard on shoulder, back to his lighted den.

"Taheia, here to my side!"—"Rua, my Rua, you!"

And cold from the clutch of terror, cold with the damp of the dew,

Taheia, heavy of hair, leaped through the dark to his arms;

Taheia leaped to his clasp, and was folded in from alarms.

"Rua, beloved, here, see what your love has brought;

Coming—alas! returning—swift as the shuttle of thought;

Returning, alas! for to-night, with the beaten drum and the voice,

In the shine of many torches must the sleepless clan rejoice;

And Taheia the well-descended, the daughter of chief and priest,

Taheia must sit in her place in the crowded bench of the feast."

So it was spoken; and she, girding her garment high,

Fled and was swallowed of woods, swift as the sight of an eye.

Night over isle and sea rolled her curtain of stars,

Then a trouble awoke in the air, the east was banded with bars;

Dawn as yellow as sulphur leaped on the mountain height;

Dawn, in the deepest glen, fell a wonder of light;

High and clear stood the palms in the eye of the brightening east,

And lo! from the sides of the sea the broken sound of the feast!

As, when in days of summer, through open windows, the fly

Swift as a breeze and loud as a trump goes by,

But when frosts in the field have pinched the wintering mouse,

Blindly noses and buzzes and hums in the firelit house:

So the sound of the feast gallantly trampled at night,

So it staggered and drooped, and droned in the morning light.

IV. THE RAID

It chanced that as Rua sat in the valley of silent falls,

He heard a calling of doves from high on the cliffy walls.

Fire had fashioned of yore, and time had broken, the rocks;

There were rooting crannies for trees and nesting-places for flocks;

And he saw on the top of the cliffs, looking up from the pit of the shade,

A flicker of wings and sunshine, and trees that swung in the trade.

"The trees swing in the trade," quoth Rua, doubtful of words,

"And the sun stares from the sky, but what should trouble the birds?"

Up from the shade he gazed, where high the parapet shone,

And he was aware of a ledge and of things that moved thereon.

"What manner of things are these? Are they spirits abroad by day?

Or the foes of my clan that are come, bringing death by a perilous way?"

The valley was gouged like a vessel, and round like the vessel's lip,

With a cape of the side of the hill thrust forth like the bows of a ship.

On the top of the face of the cape a volley of sun struck fair,

And the cape overhung like a chin a gulph of sunless air.

"Silence, heart! What is that?—that, that flickered and shone,

Into the sun for an instant, and in an instant gone?

Was it a warrior's plume, a warrior's girdle of hair?

Swung in the loop of a rope, is he making a bridge of the air?"

Once and again Rua saw, in the trenchant edge of the sky,

The giddy conjuring done. And then, in the blink of an eye,

A scream caught in with the breath, a whirling packet of limbs,

A lump that dived in the gulph, more swift than a dolphin swims;

And there was the lump at his feet, and eyes were alive in the lump.

Sick was the soul of Rua, ambushed close in a clump;

Sick of soul he drew near, making his courage stout;

And he looked in the face of the thing, and the life of the thing went out.

And he gazed on the tattooed limbs, and, behold, he knew the man:

Hoka, a chief of the Vais, the truculent foe of his clan:

Hoka a moment since that stepped in the loop of the rope,

Filled with the lust of war, and alive with courage and hope.

Again to the giddy cornice Rua lifted his eyes,

And again beheld men passing in the armpit of the skies.

"Foes of my race!" cried Rua, "the mouth of Rua is true:

Never a shark in the deep is nobler of soul than you.

There was never a nobler foray, never a bolder plan;

Never a dizzier path was trod by the children of man;

And Rua, your evil-dealer through all the days of his years,

"Counts it honour to hate you, honour to fall by your spears."

And Rua straightened his back. "O Vais, a scheme for a scheme!"

Cried Rua and turned and descended the turbulent stair of the stream,

Leaping from rock to rock as the water-wagtail at home

Flits through resonant valleys and skims by boulder and foam.

And Rua burst from the glen and leaped on the shore of the brook,

And straight for the roofs of the clan his vigorous way he took.

Swift were the heels of his flight, and loud behind as he went

Rattled the leaping stones on the line of his long descent.

And ever he thought as he ran, and caught at his gasping breath,

"O the fool of a Rua, Rua that runs to his death!

But the right is the right," thought Rua, and ran like the wind on the foam,

"The right is the right for ever, and home for ever home.

For what though the oven smoke? And what though I die ere morn?

There was I nourished and tended, and there was Taheia born."

Noon was high on the High-place, the second noon of the feast;

And heat and shameful slumber weighed on people and priest;

And the heart drudged slow in bodies heavy with monstrous meals;

And the senseless limbs were scattered abroad like spokes of wheels;

And crapulous women sat and stared at the stones anigh

With a bestial droop of the lip and a swinish rheum in the eye.

As about the dome of the bees in the time for the drones to fall,

The dead and the maimed are scattered, and lie, and stagger, and crawl;

So on the grades of the terrace, in the ardent eye of the day,

The half-awake and the sleepers clustered and crawled and lay;

And loud as the dome of the bees, in the time of a swarming horde,

A horror of many insects hung in the air and roared.

Rua looked and wondered; he said to himself in his heart:

"Poor are the pleasures of life, and death is the better part."

But lo! on the higher benches a cluster of tranquil folk

Sat by themselves, nor raised their serious eyes, nor spoke:

Women with robes unruffled and garlands duly arranged,

Gazing far from the feast with faces of people estranged;

And quiet amongst the quiet, and fairer than all the fair,

Taheia, the well-descended, Taheia, heavy of hair.

And the soul of Rua awoke, courage enlightened his eyes,

And he uttered a summoning shout and called on the clan to rise.

Over against him at once, in the spotted shade of the trees,

Owlish and blinking creatures scrambled to hands and knees;

On the grades of the sacred terrace, the driveller woke to fear,

And the hand of the ham-drooped warrior brandished a wavering spear.

And Rua folded his arms, and scorn discovered his teeth;

Above the war-crowd gibbered, and Rua stood smiling beneath.

Thick, like leaves in the autumn, faint, like April sleet,

Missiles from tremulous hands quivered around his feet;

And Taheia leaped from her place; and the priest, the ruby-eyed,

Ran to the front of the terrace, and brandished his arms, and cried:

"Hold, O fools, he brings tidings!" and "Hold, 'tis the love of my heart!"

Till lo! in front of the terrace, Rua pierced with a dart.

Taheia cherished his head, and the aged priest stood by,

And gazed with eyes of ruby at Rua's darkening eye.

"Taheia, here is the end, I die a death for a man.

I have given the life of my soul to save an unsavable clan.

See them, the drooping of hams! behold me the blinking crew:

Fifty spears they cast, and one of fifty true!

And you, O priest, the foreteller, foretell for yourself if you can,

Foretell the hour of the day when the Vais shall burst on your clan!

By the head of the tapu cleft, with death and fire in their hand,

Thick and silent like ants, the warriors swarm in the land."

And they tell that when next the sun had climbed to the noonday skies,

It shone on the smoke of feasting in the country of the Vais.

NOTES TO THE FEAST OF FAMINE

In this ballad, I have strung together some of the more striking particularities of the Marquesas. It rests upon no authority; it is in no sense, like "Rahéro," a native story; but a patchwork of details of manners and the impressions of a traveller. It may seem strange, when the scene is laid upon these profligate islands, to make the story hinge on love. But love is not less known in the Marquesas than elsewhere; nor is there any cause of suicide more common in the islands.

[61] Note 1. "Pit of Popoi." Where the breadfruit was stored for preservation.

[62a] Note 2. "Ruby-red." The priest's eyes were probably red from the abuse of kava. His beard (ib.) is said to be worth an estate; for the beards of old men are the favourite head adornment of the Marquesans, as the hair of women formed their most costly girdle. The former, among this generally beardless and short-lived people, fetch to-day considerable sums.

[62b] Note 3. "Tikis." The tiki is an ugly image hewn out of wood or stone.

[67] Note 4. "The one-stringed harp." Usually employed for serenades.

[69] Note 5. "The sacred cabin of palm." Which, however, no woman could approach. I do not know where women were tattooed; probably in the common house, or in the bush, for a woman was a creature of small account. I must guard the reader against supposing Taheia was at all disfigured; the art of the Marquesan tattooer is extreme; and she would appear to be clothed in a web of lace, inimitably delicate, exquisite in pattern, and of a bluish hue that at once contrasts and harmonises with the warm pigment of the native skin. It would be hard to find a woman more becomingly adorned than "a well-tattooed" Marquesan.

[72] Note 6. "The horror of night." The Polynesian fear of ghosts and of the dark has been already referred to. Their life is beleaguered by the dead.

[74] Note 7. "The quiet passage of souls." So, I am told, the natives explain the sound of a little wind passing overhead unfelt.

[78] Note 8. "The first of the victims fell." Without doubt, this whole scene is untrue to fact. The victims were disposed of privately and some time before. And indeed I am far from claiming the credit of any high degree of accuracy for this ballad. Even in a time of famine, it is probable that Marquesan life went far more gaily than is here represented. But the melancholy of to-day lies on the writer's mind.

TICONDEROGA: A LEGEND OF THE WEST HIGHLANDS

TICONDEROGA

This is the tale of the man
  Who heard a word in the night
In the land of the heathery hills,
  In the days of the feud and the fight.
By the sides of the rainy sea,
  Where never a stranger came,
On the awful lips of the dead,
  He heard the outlandish name.
It sang in his sleeping ears,
  It hummed in his waking head:
The name—Ticonderoga,
  The utterance of the dead.

I. THE SAYING OF THE NAME

On the loch-sides of Appin,

    When the mist blew from the sea,

A Stewart stood with a Cameron:

    An angry man was he.

The blood beat in his ears,

    The blood ran hot to his head,

The mist blew from the sea,

    And there was the Cameron dead.

"O, what have I done to my friend,

    O, what have I done to mysel',

That he should be cold and dead,

    And I in the danger of all?

Nothing but danger about me,

    Danger behind and before,

Death at wait in the heather

    In Appin and Mamore,

Hate at all of the ferries

    And death at each of the fords,

Camerons priming gunlocks

    And Camerons sharpening swords."

But this was a man of counsel,

   This was a man of a score,

There dwelt no pawkier Stewart

   In Appin or Mamore.

He looked on the blowing mist,

   He looked on the awful dead,

And there came a smile on his face

   And there slipped a thought in his head.

Out over cairn and moss,

   Out over scrog and scaur,

He ran as runs the clansman

   That bears the cross of war.

His heart beat in his body,

   His hair clove to his face,

When he came at last in the gloaming

   To the dead man's brother's place.

The east was white with the moon,

   The west with the sun was red,

And there, in the house-doorway,

   Stood the brother of the dead.

"I have slain a man to my danger,

I have slain a man to my death.

I put my soul in your hands,"

    The panting Stewart saith.

"I lay it bare in your hands,

    For I know your hands are leal;

And be you my targe and bulwark

    From the bullet and the steel."

Then up and spoke the Cameron,

    And gave him his hand again:

"There shall never a man in Scotland

    Set faith in me in vain;

And whatever man you have slaughtered,

    Of whatever name or line,

By my sword and yonder mountain,

    I make your quarrel mine. [103]

I bid you in to my fireside,

    I share with you house and hall;

It stands upon my honour

    To see you safe from all."

It fell in the time of midnight,

    When the fox barked in the den

And the plaids were over the faces
   In all the houses of men,
That as the living Cameron
   Lay sleepless on his bed,
Out of the night and the other world,
   Came in to him the dead.

"My blood is on the heather,
   My bones are on the hill;
There is joy in the home of ravens
   That the young shall eat their fill.
My blood is poured in the dust,
   My soul is spilled in the air;
And the man that has undone me
   Sleeps in my brother's care."

"I'm wae for your death, my brother,
   But if all of my house were dead,
I couldnae withdraw the plighted hand,
   Nor break the word once said."

"O, what shall I say to our father,
   In the place to which I fare?

O, what shall I say to our mother,

　Who greets to see me there?

And to all the kindly Camerons

　That have lived and died long-syne—

Is this the word you send them,

　Fause-hearted brother mine?"

"It's neither fear nor duty,

　It's neither quick nor dead

Shall gar me withdraw the plighted hand,

　Or break the word once said."

Thrice in the time of midnight,

　When the fox barked in the den,

And the plaids were over the faces

　In all the houses of men,

Thrice as the living Cameron

　Lay sleepless on his bed,

Out of the night and the other world

　Came in to him the dead,

And cried to him for vengeance

　On the man that laid him low;

And thrice the living Cameron

Told the dead Cameron, no.

"Thrice have you seen me, brother,
　　But now shall see me no more,
Till you meet your angry fathers
　　Upon the farther shore.
Thrice have I spoken, and now,
　　Before the cock be heard,
I take my leave for ever
　　With the naming of a word.
It shall sing in your sleeping ears,
　　It shall hum in your waking head,
The name—Ticonderoga,
　　And the warning of the dead."

Now when the night was over
　　And the time of people's fears,
The Cameron walked abroad,
　　And the word was in his ears.
"Many a name I know,
　　But never a name like this;
O, where shall I find a skilly man
　　Shall tell me what it is?"

With many a man he counselled

    Of high and low degree,

With the herdsmen on the mountains

    And the fishers of the sea.

And he came and went unweary,

    And read the books of yore,

And the runes that were written of old

    On stones upon the moor.

And many a name he was told,

    But never the name of his fears—

Never, in east or west,

    The name that rang in his ears:

Names of men and of clans;

    Names for the grass and the tree,

For the smallest tarn in the mountains,

    The smallest reef in the sea:

Names for the high and low,

    The names of the craig and the flat;

But in all the land of Scotland,

    Never a name like that.

II. THE SEEKING OF THE NAME

And now there was speech in the south,

  And a man of the south that was wise,

A periwig'd lord of London, [109]

  Called on the clans to rise.

And the riders rode, and the summons

  Came to the western shore,

To the land of the sea and the heather,

  To Appin and Mamore.

It called on all to gather

  From every scrog and scaur,

That loved their fathers' tartan

  And the ancient game of war.

And down the watery valley

  And up the windy hill,

Once more, as in the olden,

  The pipes were sounding shrill;

Again in highland sunshine

  The naked steel was bright;

And the lads, once more in tartan

  Went forth again to fight.

"O, why should I dwell here

   With a weird upon my life,

When the clansmen shout for battle

   And the war-swords clash in strife?

I cannae joy at feast,

   I cannae sleep in bed,

For the wonder of the word

   And the warning of the dead.

It sings in my sleeping ears,

   It hums in my waking head,

The name—Ticonderoga,

   The utterance of the dead.

Then up, and with the fighting men

   To march away from here,

Till the cry of the great war-pipe

   Shall drown it in my ear!"

Where flew King George's ensign

   The plaided soldiers went:

They drew the sword in Germany,

   In Flanders pitched the tent.

The bells of foreign cities

Rang far across the plain:

They passed the happy Rhine,

They drank the rapid Main.

Through Asiatic jungles

The Tartans filed their way,

And the neighing of the war-pipes

Struck terror in Cathay. [111]

"Many a name have I heard," he thought,

"In all the tongues of men,

Full many a name both here and there.

Full many both now and then.

When I was at home in my father's house

In the land of the naked knee,

Between the eagles that fly in the lift

And the herrings that swim in the sea,

And now that I am a captain-man

With a braw cockade in my hat—

Many a name have I heard," he thought,

"But never a name like that."

III. THE PLACE OF THE NAME

There fell a war in a woody place,
  Lay far across the sea,
A war of the march in the mirk midnight
  And the shot from behind the tree,
The shaven head and the painted face,
  The silent foot in the wood,
In a land of a strange, outlandish tongue
  That was hard to be understood.

It fell about the gloaming
  The general stood with his staff,
He stood and he looked east and west
  With little mind to laugh.
"Far have I been and much have I seen,
  And kent both gain and loss,
But here we have woods on every hand
  And a kittle water to cross.
Far have I been and much have I seen,
  But never the beat of this;
And there's one must go down to that waterside
  To see how deep it is."

It fell in the dusk of the night
    When unco things betide,
The skilly captain, the Cameron,
    Went down to that waterside.
Canny and soft the captain went;
    And a man of the woody land,
With the shaven head and the painted face,
    Went down at his right hand.
It fell in the quiet night,
    There was never a sound to ken;
But all of the woods to the right and the left
    Lay filled with the painted men.

"Far have I been and much have I seen,
    Both as a man and boy,
But never have I set forth a foot
    On so perilous an employ."
It fell in the dusk of the night
    When unco things betide,
That he was aware of a captain-man
    Drew near to the waterside.
He was aware of his coming

Down in the gloaming alone;

And he looked in the face of the man

And lo! the face was his own.

"This is my weird," he said,

"And now I ken the worst;

For many shall fall the morn,

But I shall fall with the first.

O, you of the outland tongue,

You of the painted face,

This is the place of my death;

Can you tell me the name of the place?"

"Since the Frenchmen have been here

They have called it Sault-Marie;

But that is a name for priests,

And not for you and me.

It went by another word,"

Quoth he of the shaven head:

"It was called Ticonderoga

In the days of the great dead."

And it fell on the morrow's morning,

In the fiercest of the fight,

That the Cameron bit the dust

As he foretold at night;

And far from the hills of heather

Far from the isles of the sea,

He sleeps in the place of the name

As it was doomed to be.

NOTES TO TICONDEROGA

Introduction.—I first heard this legend of my own country from that friend of men of letters, Mr. Alfred Nutt, "there in roaring London's central stream," and since the ballad first saw the light of day in Scribner's Magazine, Mr. Nutt and Lord Archibald Campbell have been in public controversy on the facts. Two clans, the Camerons and the Campbells, lay claim to this bracing story; and they do well: the man who preferred his plighted troth to the commands and menaces of the dead is an ancestor worth disputing. But the Campbells must rest content: they have the broad lands and the broad page of history; this appanage must be denied them; for between the name of Cameron and that of Campbell, the muse will never hesitate.

[103] Note 1. Mr. Nutt reminds me it was "by my sword and Ben Cruachan" the Cameron swore.

[109] Note 2. "A periwig'd lord of London." The first Pitt.

[111] Note 3. "Cathay." There must be some omission in General Stewart's charming History of the Highland Regiments, a book that might well be republished and continued; or it scarce appears how our friend could have got to China.

HEATHER ALE: A GALLOWAY LEGEND

HEATHER ALE

From the bonny bells of heather
   They brewed a drink long-syne,
Was sweeter far than honey,
   Was stronger far than wine.
They brewed it and they drank it,
   And lay in a blessed swound
For days and days together
   In their dwellings underground.

There rose a king in Scotland,
   A fell man to his foes,
He smote the Picts in battle,
   He hunted them like roes.
Over miles of the red mountain
   He hunted as they fled,
And strewed the dwarfish bodies
   Of the dying and the dead.

Summer came in the country,

    Red was the heather bell;

But the manner of the brewing

    Was none alive to tell.

In graves that were like children's

    On many a mountain head,

The Brewsters of the Heather

    Lay numbered with the dead.

The king in the red moorland

    Rode on a summer's day;

And the bees hummed, and the curlews

    Cried beside the way.

The king rode, and was angry,

    Black was his brow and pale,

To rule in a land of heather

    And lack the Heather Ale.

It fortuned that his vassals,

    Riding free on the heath,

Came on a stone that was fallen

    And vermin hid beneath.

    Rudely plucked from their hiding,

Never a word they spoke:

A son and his aged father—

Last of the dwarfish folk.

The king sat high on his charger,

He looked on the little men;

And the dwarfish and swarthy couple

Looked at the king again.

Down by the shore he had them;

And there on the giddy brink—

"I will give you life, ye vermin,

For the secret of the drink."

There stood the son and father

And they looked high and low;

The heather was red around them,

The sea rumbled below.

And up and spoke the father,

Shrill was his voice to hear:

"I have a word in private,

A word for the royal ear.

"Life is dear to the aged,

And honour a little thing;

I would gladly sell the secret,"

Quoth the Pict to the King.

His voice was small as a sparrow's,

And shrill and wonderful clear:

"I would gladly sell my secret,

Only my son I fear.

"For life is a little matter,

And death is nought to the young;

And I dare not sell my honour

Under the eye of my son.

Take him, O king, and bind him,

And cast him far in the deep;

And it's I will tell the secret

That I have sworn to keep."

They took the son and bound him,

Neck and heels in a thong,

And a lad took him and swung him,

And flung him far and strong,

And the sea swallowed his body,

Like that of a child of ten;—

And there on the cliff stood the father,

    Last of the dwarfish men.

"True was the word I told you:

    Only my son I feared;

For I doubt the sapling courage

    That goes without the beard.

But now in vain is the torture,

    Fire shall never avail:

Here dies in my bosom

    The secret of Heather Ale."

NOTE TO HEATHER ALE

Among the curiosities of human nature, this legend claims a high place. It is needless to remind the reader that the Picts were never exterminated, and form to this day a large proportion of the folk of Scotland: occupying the eastern and the central parts, from the Firth of Forth, or perhaps the Lammermoors, upon the south, to the Ord of Caithness on the north. That the blundering guess of a dull chronicler should have inspired men with imaginary loathing for their own ancestors is already strange: that it should have begotten this wild legend seems incredible. Is it possible the chronicler's error was merely nominal? that what he told, and what the people proved themselves so ready to receive, about the Picts, was true or partly true of some anterior and perhaps Lappish savages, small of stature, black of hue, dwelling underground—possibly also the distillers of some forgotten spirit? See Mr. Campbell's Tales of the West Highlands.

CHRISTMAS AT SEA

The sheets were frozen hard, and they cut the naked hand;

The decks were like a slide, where a seaman scarce could stand;

The wind was a nor'wester, blowing squally off the sea;

And cliffs and spouting breakers were the only things a-lee.

They heard the surf a-roaring before the break of day;

But 'twas only with the peep of light we saw how ill we lay.

We tumbled every hand on deck instanter, with a shout,

And we gave her the maintops'l, and stood by to go about.

All day we tacked and tacked between the South Head and the North;

All day we hauled the frozen sheets, and got no further forth;

All day as cold as charity, in bitter pain and dread,

For very life and nature we tacked from head to head.

We gave the South a wider berth, for there the tide-race roared;

But every tack we made we brought the North Head close aboard:

So's we saw the cliffs and houses, and the breakers running high,

And the coastguard in his garden, with his glass against his eye.

The frost was on the village roofs as white as ocean foam;

The good red fires were burning bright in every 'longshore home;

The windows sparkled clear, and the chimneys volleyed out;

And I vow we sniffed the victuals as the vessel went about.

The bells upon the church were rung with a mighty jovial cheer;

For it's just that I should tell you how (of all days in the year)

This day of our adversity was blessèd Christmas morn,

And the house above the coastguard's was the house where I was born.

O well I saw the pleasant room, the pleasant faces there,

My mother's silver spectacles, my father's silver hair;

And well I saw the firelight, like a flight of homely elves,

Go dancing round the china-plates that stand upon the shelves.

And well I knew the talk they had, the talk that was of me,

Of the shadow on the household and the son that went to sea;

And O the wicked fool I seemed, in every kind of way,

To be here and hauling frozen ropes on blessèd Christmas Day.

They lit the high sea-light, and the dark began to fall.

"All hands to loose topgallant sails," I heard the captain call.

"By the Lord, she'll never stand it," our first mate, Jackson, cried.

. . . "It's the one way or the other, Mr. Jackson," he replied.

She staggered to her bearings, but the sails were new and good,

And the ship smelt up to windward just as though she understood.

As the winter's day was ending, in the entry of the night,

We cleared the weary headland, and passed below the light.

And they heaved a mighty breath, every soul on board but me,

As they saw her nose again pointing handsome out to sea;

But all that I could think of, in the darkness and the cold,

Was just that I was leaving home and my folks were growing old.

THE END

About Author

Childhood and youth

Stevenson was born at 8 Howard Place, Edinburgh, Scotland on 13 November 1850 to Thomas Stevenson (1818–87), a leading lighthouse engineer, and his wife Margaret Isabella (born Balfour, 1829–97). He was christened Robert Lewis Balfour Stevenson. At about age 18, he changed the spelling of "Lewis" to "Louis", and he dropped "Balfour" in 1873.

Lighthouse design was the family's profession; Thomas's father (Robert's grandfather) was civil engineer Robert Stevenson, and Thomas's brothers (Robert's uncles) Alan and David were in the same field. Thomas's maternal grandfather Thomas Smith had been in the same profession. However, Robert's mother's family were gentry, tracing their lineage back to Alexander Balfour who had held the lands of Inchyra in Fife in the fifteenth century. His mother's father Lewis Balfour (1777–1860) was a minister of the Church of Scotland at nearby Colinton, and her siblings included physician George William Balfour and marine engineer James Balfour. Stevenson spent the greater part of his boyhood holidays in his maternal grandfather's house. "Now I often wonder what I inherited from this old minister," Stevenson wrote. "I must suppose, indeed, that he was fond of preaching sermons, and so am I, though I never heard it maintained that either of us loved to hear them."

Lewis Balfour and his daughter both had weak chests, so they often needed to stay in warmer climates for their health. Stevenson inherited a tendency to coughs and fevers, exacerbated when the family moved to a damp, chilly house at 1 Inverleith Terrace in 1851. The family moved again to the sunnier 17 Heriot Row when Stevenson was six years old, but the tendency to extreme sickness in winter remained with him until he was 11. Illness was a recurrent feature of his adult life and left him extraordinarily thin. Contemporaneous views were that he had tuberculosis, but more recent views are that it was bronchiectasis or even sarcoidosis.

Stevenson's parents were both devout Presbyterians, but the household was not strict in its adherence to Calvinist principles. His nurse Alison Cunningham (known as Cummy) was more fervently religious. Her mix of Calvinism and folk beliefs were an early source of nightmares for the child, and he showed a precocious concern for religion. But she also cared for him tenderly in illness, reading to him from John Bunyan and the Bible as he lay sick in bed and telling tales of the Covenanters. Stevenson recalled this time of sickness in "The Land of Counterpane" in A Child's Garden of Verses (1885), dedicating the book to his nurse.

Stevenson was an only child, both strange-looking and eccentric, and he found it hard to fit in when he was sent to a nearby school at age 6, a problem repeated at age 11 when he went on to the Edinburgh Academy; but he mixed well in lively games with his cousins in summer holidays at Colinton. His frequent illnesses often kept him away from his first school, so he was taught for long stretches by private tutors. He was a late reader, learning at age 7 or 8, but even before this he dictated stories to his mother and nurse, and he compulsively wrote stories throughout his childhood. His father was proud of this interest; he had also written stories in his spare time until his own father found them and told him to "give up such nonsense and mind your business." He paid for the printing of Robert's first publication at 16, entitled The Pentland Rising: A Page of History, 1666. It was an account of the Covenanters' rebellion which was published in 1866, the 200th anniversary of the event.

Education

In September 1857, Stevenson went to Mr Henderson's School in India Street, Edinburgh, but because of poor health stayed only a few weeks and did not return until October 1859. During his many absences he was taught by private tutors. In October 1861, he went to Edinburgh Academy, an independent school for boys, and stayed there sporadically for about fifteen months. In the autumn of 1863, he spent one term at an English boarding school at Spring Grove in Isleworth in Middlesex (now an urban area of West London). In October 1864, following an improvement to his health, he was sent to Robert Thomson's private school in Frederick Street, Edinburgh, where he remained until he went to university. In November 1867, Stevenson entered the University of Edinburgh to study engineering. He showed from the start no enthusiasm for his studies and devoted much energy to avoiding lectures. This time was more important for the friendships he made with other students in the Speculative Society (an exclusive debating club), particularly with Charles Baxter, who would become Stevenson's financial agent, and with a professor, Fleeming Jenkin, whose house staged amateur drama in which Stevenson took part, and whose biography he would later write. Perhaps most important at this point in his life was a cousin, Robert Alan Mowbray Stevenson (known as "Bob"), a lively and light-hearted young man who, instead of the family profession, had chosen to study art. Each year during vacations, Stevenson travelled to inspect the family's engineering works—to Anstruther and Wick in 1868, with his father on his official tour of Orkney and Shetland islands lighthouses in 1869, and for three weeks to the island of Erraid in 1870. He enjoyed the travels more for the material they gave for his writing than for any engineering interest. The voyage with his father pleased him because a similar journey of Walter Scott with Robert Stevenson had provided the inspiration for Scott's 1822 novel The Pirate. In April 1871, Stevenson notified his father of his decision to pursue a life of letters. Though the elder Stevenson was naturally disappointed, the surprise cannot have been great, and Stevenson's mother reported that he was "wonderfully resigned" to his son's choice. To provide some security, it was agreed that Stevenson should read Law (again at Edinburgh University) and be called to the Scottish bar. In his 1887 poetry collection Underwoods, Stevenson muses on his having turned from the family profession:

Say not of me that weakly I declined

The labours of my sires, and fled the sea,

The towers we founded and the lamps we lit,

To play at home with paper like a child.

But rather say: In the afternoon of time

A strenuous family dusted from its hands

The sand of granite, and beholding far

Along the sounding coast its pyramids

And tall memorials catch the dying sun,

Smiled well content, and to this childish task

Around the fire addressed its evening hours.

In other respects too, Stevenson was moving away from his upbringing. His dress became more Bohemian; he already wore his hair long, but he now took to wearing a velveteen jacket and rarely attended parties in conventional evening dress. Within the limits of a strict allowance, he visited cheap pubs and brothels. More importantly, he had come to reject Christianity and declared himself an atheist. In January 1873, his father came across the constitution of the LJR (Liberty, Justice, Reverence) Club, of which Stevenson and his cousin Bob were members, which began: "Disregard everything our parents have taught us". Questioning his son about his beliefs, he discovered the truth, leading to a long period of dissension with both parents:

What a damned curse I am to my parents! As my father said "You have rendered my whole life a failure". As my mother said "This is the heaviest affliction that has ever befallen me". O Lord, what a pleasant thing it is to have damned the happiness of (probably) the only two people who care a damn about you in the world.

Early writing and travels

Stevenson was visiting a cousin in England in late 1873 when he met two people who became very important to him: Sidney Colvin and Fanny (Frances Jane) Sitwell. Sitwell was a 34-year-old woman with a son, who was separated from her husband. She attracted the devotion of many who met her, including Colvin, who married her in 1901. Stevenson was also drawn to her, and they kept up a warm correspondence over several years in which he wavered between the role of a suitor and a son (he addressed her as "Madonna"). Colvin became Stevenson's literary adviser and was the first editor of his letters after his death. He placed Stevenson's first paid contribution in The Portfolio, an essay entitled "Roads".

Stevenson was soon active in London literary life, becoming acquainted with many of the writers of the time, including Andrew Lang, Edmund Gosse, and Leslie Stephen, the editor of the Cornhill Magazine who took an interest in Stevenson's work. Stephen took Stevenson to visit a patient at the Edinburgh Infirmary named William Ernest Henley, an energetic and talkative man with a wooden leg. Henley became a close friend and occasional literary collaborator, until a quarrel broke up the friendship in 1888, and he is often considered to be the model for Long John Silver in Treasure Island.

Stevenson was sent to Menton on the French Riviera in November 1873 to recuperate after his health failed. He returned in better health in April 1874 and settled down to his studies, but he returned to France several times after that. He made long and frequent trips to the neighborhood of the Forest of Fontainebleau, staying at Barbizon, Grez-sur-Loing, and Nemours and becoming a member of the artists' colonies there. He also traveled to Paris to visit galleries and the theatres. He qualified for the Scottish bar in July 1875, and his father added a brass plate to the Heriot Row house reading "R.L. Stevenson, Advocate". His law studies did influence his books, but he never practised law; all his energies were spent in travel and writing. One of his journeys was a canoe voyage in Belgium and France with Sir Walter Simpson, a friend from the Speculative Society, a frequent travel companion, and the author of The Art of Golf (1887). This trip was the basis of his first travel book An Inland Voyage (1878).

Marriage

The canoe voyage with Simpson brought Stevenson to Grez in September 1876 where he met Fanny Van de Grift Osbourne (1840–1914), born in Indianapolis. She had married at age 17 and moved to Nevada to rejoin husband Samuel after his participation in the American Civil War. Their children were Isobel (or "Belle"), Lloyd, and Hervey (who died in 1875). But anger over her husband's infidelities led to a number of separations. In 1875, she had taken her children to France where she and Isobel studied art.

Stevenson returned to Britain shortly after this first meeting, but Fanny apparently remained in his thoughts, and he wrote the essay "On falling in love" for the Cornhill Magazine. They met again early in 1877 and became lovers. Stevenson spent much of the following year with her and her children in France. In August 1878, she returned to San Francisco and Stevenson remained in Europe, making the walking trip that formed the basis for Travels with a Donkey in the Cévennes (1879). But he set off to join her in August 1879, against the advice of his friends and without notifying his parents. He took second-class passage on the steamship Devonia, in part to save money but also to learn how others traveled and to increase the adventure of the journey. He then traveled overland by train from New York City to California. He later wrote about the experience in The Amateur Emigrant. It was good experience for his writing, but it broke his health.

He was near death when he arrived in Monterey, California, where some local ranchers nursed him back to health. He stayed for a time at the French Hotel located at 530 Houston Street, now a museum dedicated to his memory called the "Stevenson House". While there, he often dined "on the cuff," as he said, at a nearby restaurant run by Frenchman Jules Simoneau which stood at what is now Simoneau Plaza; several years later, he sent Simoneau an inscribed copy of his novel Strange Case of Dr Jekyll and Mr Hyde (1886), writing that it would be a stranger case still if Robert Louis Stevenson ever forgot Jules Simoneau. While in Monterey, he wrote an evocative article about "the Old Pacific Capital" of Monterey.

By December 1879, Stevenson had recovered his health enough to continue to San Francisco where he struggled "all alone on forty-five cents a day, and sometimes less, with quantities of hard work and many heavy thoughts," in an effort to support himself through his writing. But by the end of the winter, his health was broken again and he found himself at death's door. Fanny was now divorced and recovered from her own illness, and she came to his bedside and nursed him to recovery. "After a while," he wrote, "my spirit got up again in a divine frenzy, and has since kicked and spurred my vile body forward with great emphasis and success." When his father heard of his condition, he cabled him money to help him through this period.

Fanny and Robert were married in May 1880, although he said that he was "a mere complication of cough and bones, much fitter for an emblem of mortality than a bridegroom." He travelled with his new wife and her son Lloyd north of San Francisco to Napa Valley and spent a summer honeymoon at an abandoned mining camp on Mount Saint Helena. He wrote about this experience in The Silverado Squatters. He met Charles Warren Stoddard, co-editor of the Overland Monthly and author of South Sea Idylls, who urged Stevenson to travel to the South Pacific, an idea which returned to him many years later. In August 1880, he sailed with Fanny and Lloyd from New York to Britain and found his parents and his friend Sidney Colvin on the wharf at Liverpool, happy to see him return home. Gradually, his wife was able to patch up differences between father and son and make herself a part of the family through her charm and wit.

Attempted settlement in Europe and the US

Stevenson searched in vain between 1880 and 1887 for a residence suitable to his health. He spent his summers at various places in Scotland and England, including Westbourne, Dorset, a residential area in Bournemouth. It was during his time in Bournemouth that he wrote the story Strange Case of Dr Jekyll and Mr Hyde, naming the character Mr. Poole after the town of Poole which is situated next to Bournemouth. In Westbourne, he named his house Skerryvore after the tallest lighthouse in Scotland, which his uncle Alan had built (1838–44). In the wintertime, Stevenson travelled to France and lived at Davos Platz and the Chalet de Solitude at Hyères, where he was very happy for a time. "I have so many things to make life sweet for me," he wrote, "it seems a pity I cannot have that other one thing—health. But though you will be angry to hear it, I believe, for myself at least, what is is best." In spite of his ill health, he produced the bulk of his best-known work during these years. Treasure Island was published under the pseudonym "Captain George North" and became his first widely popular book; he wrote it during this time, along with Kidnapped, Strange Case of Dr Jekyll and Mr Hyde (which established his wider reputation), The Black Arrow: A Tale of the Two Roses, A Child's Garden of Verses, and Underwoods. He gave a copy of Kidnapped to his friend and frequent Skerryvore visitor Henry James.

His father died in 1887 and Stevenson felt free to follow the advice of his physician to try a complete change of climate, so he headed for Colorado with his mother and family. But after landing in New York, they decided to spend the winter in the Adirondacks at a cure cottage now known as Stevenson Cottage at Saranac Lake, New York. During the intensely cold winter, Stevenson wrote some of his best essays, including Pulvis et Umbra. He also began The Master of Ballantrae and lightheartedly planned a cruise to the southern Pacific Ocean for the following summer.

Politics

Stevenson believed in Conservatism for most of his life. His cousin and biographer Sir Graham Balfour said that "he probably throughout life would, if compelled to vote, have always supported the Conservative candidate." In 1866, Stevenson voted for Benjamin Disraeli, future Conservative Prime Minister of the United Kingdom, over Thomas Carlyle for the Lord Rectorship of the University of Edinburgh. During his college years, he briefly identified himself as a "red-hot socialist". He wrote at age 26: "I look back to the time when I was a Socialist with something like regret…. Now I know that in thus turning Conservative with years, I am going through the normal cycle of change and travelling in the common orbit of men's opinions."

Journey to the Pacific

In June 1888, Stevenson chartered the yacht Casco and set sail with his family from San Francisco. The vessel "plowed her path of snow across the empty deep, far from all track of commerce, far from any hand of help." The sea air and thrill of adventure for a time restored his health, and for nearly three years he wandered the eastern and central Pacific, stopping for extended stays at the Hawaiian Islands where he became a good friend of King Kalākaua. He befriended the king's niece Princess Victoria Kaiulani, who also had Scottish heritage. He spent time at the Gilbert Islands, Tahiti, New Zealand, and the Samoan Islands. During this period, he completed The Master of Ballantrae, composed two ballads based on the legends of the islanders, and wrote The Bottle Imp. He preserved the experience of these years in his various letters and in his In the South Seas (which was published posthumously). He made a voyage in 1889 with Lloyd on the trading schooner Equator, visiting Butaritari, Mariki, Apaiang, and Abemama in the Gilbert Islands. They spent several months on Abemama with tyrant-chief Tem Binoka, whom Stevenson described in In the South Seas.

Stevenson left Sydney on the Janet Nicoll in April 1890 for his third and final voyage among the South Seas islands. He intended to produce another book of travel writing to follow his earlier book In the South Seas, but it was his wife who eventually published her journal of their third voyage. (Fanny misnames the ship in her account The Cruise of the Janet Nichol.) A fellow passenger was Jack Buckland, whose stories of life as an island trader became the inspiration for the character of Tommy Hadden in The Wrecker (1892), which Stevenson and Lloyd Osbourne wrote together. Buckland visited the Stevensons at Vailima in 1894.

Last years

In 1890, Stevenson purchased a tract of about 400 acres (1.6 km²) in Upolu, an island in Samoa where he established himself on his estate in the village of Vailima after two aborted attempts to visit Scotland. He took the native name Tusitala (Samoan for "Teller of Tales"). His influence spread among the Samoans, who consulted him for advice, and he soon became involved in local politics. He was convinced that the European officials who had been appointed to rule the Samoans were incompetent, and he published A Footnote to History after many futile attempts to resolve the matter. This was such a stinging protest against existing conditions that it resulted in the recall of two officials, and Stevenson feared for a time that it would result in his own deportation. He wrote to Colvin, "I used to think meanly of the plumber; but how he shines beside the politician!"

He also found time to work at his writing, although he felt that "there was never any man had so many irons in the fire". He wrote The Beach of Falesa, Catriona (titled David Balfour in the US), The Ebb-Tide, and the Vailima Letters during this period.

Stevenson grew depressed and wondered if he had exhausted his creative vein, as he had been "overworked bitterly" and that the best he could write was "ditch-water". He even feared that he might again become a helpless invalid. He rebelled against this idea: "I wish to die in my boots; no more Land of Counterpane for me. To be drowned, to be shot, to be thrown from a horse — ay, to be hanged, rather than pass again through that slow dissolution." He then suddenly had a return of energy and he began work on Weir of Hermiston. "It's so good that it frightens me," he is reported to have exclaimed. He felt that this was the best work he had done.

On 3 December 1894, Stevenson was talking to his wife and straining to open a bottle of wine when he suddenly exclaimed, "What's that?", asked his wife "does my face look strange?", and collapsed. He died within a few hours, probably of a cerebral haemorrhage. He was 44 years old. The Samoans insisted on surrounding his body with a watch-guard during the night and on bearing him on their shoulders to nearby Mount Vaea, where they buried him on a spot overlooking the sea on land donated by British Acting Vice Consul Thomas Trood. Stevenson had always wanted his Requiem inscribed on his tomb:

Under the wide and starry sky,

Dig the grave and let me lie.

Glad did I live and gladly die,

And I laid me down with a will.

This be the verse you grave for me:

Here he lies where he longed to be;

Home is the sailor, home from sea,

And the hunter home from the hill.

Stevenson was loved by the Samoans, and his tombstone epigraph was translated to a Samoan song of grief. (Source: Wikipedia)

9 789389 370683